SUSAN L. ROTH

Buddha

A DOUBLEDAY BOOK FOR YOUNG READERS

**To M. and to Lisi
with Love,**

—SWLR, M.

A Doubleday Book for Young Readers • Published by Delacorte Press • Bantam Doubleday Dell Publishing Group, Inc. • 1540 Broadway • New York, New York 10036 • Doubleday and the portrayal of an anchor with a dolphin are trademarks of Bantam Doubleday Dell Publishing Group, Inc. • Copyright © 1994 by Susan L. Roth • All rights reserved. No part of this book may be reproduced or transmitted in any form or by any means, electronic or mechanical, including photocopying, recording, or by any information storage and retrieval system, without the written permission of the Publisher, except where permitted by law. Library of Congress Cataloging in Publication Data • Roth, Susan L. Buddha / by Susan L. Roth p. cm. ISBN 0-385-31072-2 1. Gautama Buddha—Juvenile literature. [1. Buddha.] I. Title. BQ892.R68 1994 294.3'63—dc20 [B] 93-8240 CIP AC Manufactured in Italy May 1994 • 10 9 8 7 6 5 4 3 2 1

ACKNOWLEDGMENTS • I would like to thank Katherine Caldwell, Professor Emeritus of Asian Art at Mills College, Oakland, California; Lewis Lancaster, Professor of Oriental Languages and Chinese and Buddhist Studies at the University of California, Berkeley, California; Carol Bolon and Laveta Emory of the Freer/Sackler Galleries, Washington, D.C.; Denise Leidy of the Asia Society, New York, New York; His Excellency Ambassador Dr. A.W.P. Gurugé, Ambassador to the United States for the Democratic Socialist Republic of Sri Lanka for reviewing this manuscript. • I would also like to thank Sheila Swan Laufer for letting me use the papers she made with her own hands, and the Dechasiri family in Bangkok, Thailand, who made it possible for me to go to the monk in the orange robe and who showed me how to put rice into his begging bowl.—S.L.R.

Come in.

Sit down.

Cross your legs.

Take a breath.

Hum it out.

Open your hands and

listen

to the story of the

Buddha.

nce upon a lotus blossom, in the days before our grand-fathers, a beautiful queen called Maya dreamed she was carrying a milky-white elephant in her swollen belly. He stood straight and tall and held a flower in his trunk.

"You are going to have a child who will be a prince," a wise man
explained to Maya. "And one day he may become a very holy man."
And Siddhartha was born a prince, in May, under a sala tree.

Queen Maya did not live long enough even to know Siddhartha. But King Shuddhodana, Siddhartha's father, adored his son. He worried about the wise man's prediction. He wanted his son to be a happy child who would one day be king. Shuddhodana cried inside when he imagined that Siddhartha might become a holy man whose face would be lined with worry. A holy man would be a hungry, cold, and lonely man. He would deprive himself of food and clothing and friends and family, so that nothing would distract him in his search for truth. For in those days that was the way of holy men.

"It's too high a price to pay for wisdom," thought Shuddhodana. "I must keep my prince a prince. From this day on let this beautiful child see only beautiful things. Touch him only gently. Let him breathe through flowers in his garden, let his ears hear only music, let him taste only the most delicious food. Let him feel how much I love him." The baby squeezed his father's one finger with his entire tiny fist and Shuddhodana kissed the baby fingers.

Siddhartha grew princely indeed. Even though he was very young he could speak well with his elders.

He was good in his studies, handsome, and athletic. He learned to read, to write, to ride, and to shoot, though he could not learn to kill.

So Siddhartha lived, in the white palace surrounded by gardens with soft pathways for his feet, planted with every color for his eyes. He sat at laden tables, and was served only by the young and beautiful. He bathed in pools of floating flowers; young girls seated at the edges beat their drums.

Sometimes Siddhartha was curious about the world outside the palace, though when the young girls danced he forgot all but the bells on their ankles.

When Siddhartha reached sixteen, Shuddhodana still thought anxiously about the wise man's prophecy. "Siddhartha wonders about too many things. I must find someone special to delight him."

A basket was filled to the top with jewels. Young girls from every province were invited to the palace to meet the prince. Siddhartha watched his father offer precious jewels as if they were wildflowers, one to each beauty. When the basket was finally empty, one girl was still left: a girl more beautiful than all the jewels, than all the wildflowers.

"What is your name?" whispered Siddhartha. "Yashodhara," she whispered back. "Yashodhara," said Siddhartha. "May I give you my own special present?" He took the necklace from his neck and put it around hers. Yashodhara smiled into Siddhartha's eyes.

Everyone knew that Yasho-
dhara would soon be princess.
When Siddhartha and Yashodhara
were married, the celebrations
lasted seven days and seven
nights.

All this time Shuddhodana carefully protected his son from the wise man's prophecy. Siddhartha had never been outside the palace walls. He had grown even happier with Yashodhara, who was expecting their child. Finally Shuddhodana stopped worrying. He permitted Siddhartha to ride in his chariot beyond the gates.

On his first ride, Siddhartha saw a very old man. "Why is he so bent? So thin? So wrinkled?" he asked. "Old age," said the chariot driver. "It's how we all become if we're lucky enough to live so long." Siddhartha thought about the old man all the way back to the palace.

But Shuddhodana met him at the gates. They walked through the gardens and the warm breeze was touched with jasmine. The moon was a slender silver sliver. They sat at a little stone table and drank golden glasses of apricot nectar through long grass straws. The thoughts of old age were left on the other side of the palace gates.

Only much later, in the middle of the night, Siddhartha's eyes were open in the darkness. "What could I do to help that old man?" he thought. "How could I ease the weight on his poor bent legs? How can I lie contentedly on my silken cushions when he cannot even stand straight?" But when Yashodhara held him in her arms, Siddhartha sighed and fell into a gentle sleep.

The second time that Siddhartha left the palace, a sick man crossed the chariot's path; he shook with a fever and his eyes were wild. "Why does he tremble? Why is he red-eyed?" Siddhartha asked. "He's sick," said the chariot driver. "It's how we all could be if we were to breathe bad air." Siddhartha himself shivered as he thought about the sick man.

Again Shuddhodana met the chariot at the palace gates. When he saw the troubled look in Siddhartha's eyes, he put a loving hand on Siddhartha's shoulder, and led him back to the scented pools.

Siddhartha and his father played in the warm waters as if they were children. Then, wrapped in silken cloths, they ate curries with twenty-four choices of chutneys, each in its own silver dish. Siddhartha laughed with his father, but Shuddhodana worried about the empty, absent look he had seen in Siddhartha's eyes.

That night Siddhartha lay awake, remembering the sick man he had seen. "What could I do to help him? I should never have left him like that in the street. Are there others like him outside my palace walls?" Even Yashodhara's gentle beauty could not keep the sick man's face from sitting heavy in Siddhartha's heart.

The third time Siddhartha rode outside the palace walls he saw a funeral procession walking slowly along the road. "Is that a person all covered in white? Why is he lying so still, carried on high?" he asked. "He is dead," said the driver. "That is how we shall all be one day: no breathing, no thinking, no laughing, no eating, no feeling." Siddhartha tried to imagine how it would feel to be dead. He felt very frightened.

When Shuddhodana met the chariot this time, Siddhartha's eyes could hardly see. Unthinkingly he followed his father to the little stone table in the garden.

At supper Siddhartha neither ate nor spoke. Yashodhara took his hand. Her time for giving birth was very near. Although he smiled when she touched him, his eyes were hollow. All that night Siddhartha cried for the troubles of the world. Shuddhodana also cried that night. For now in his heart he could see Siddhartha clearly: skinny and hungry, gray with cold, his face lined with worry, a holy man sitting all alone.

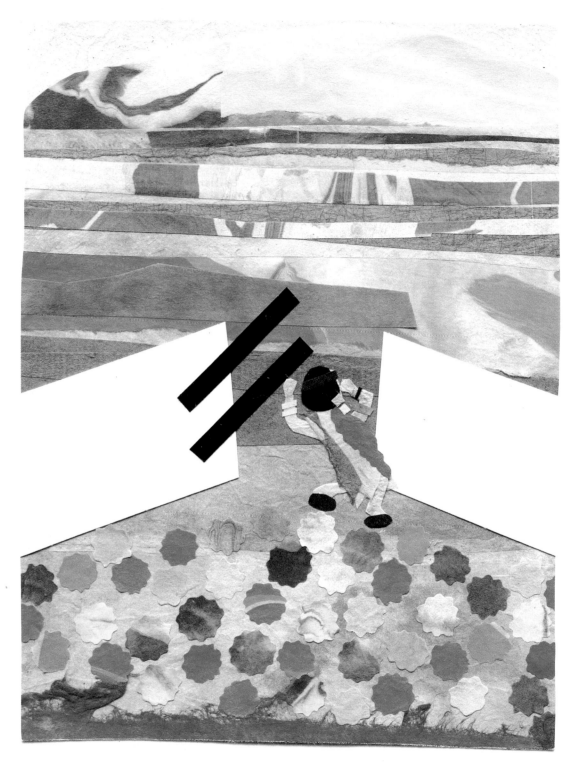

Early in the morning Shuddhodana desperately ran to the chariot driver to tell him not to leave the palace grounds again, but he was too late. Siddhartha and his driver had gone before dawn.

An orange-robed holy man was sitting quietly under a fig tree when Siddhartha took the fourth ride in his chariot. "How can you sit so calmly when old age, sickness, and death wait for everyone, even for you?" Siddhartha asked him. "How can you sit staring as if your eyes see inside yourself? Where is your fear of life?"

The holy man spoke softly. "I have thrown away my fear. I have no earthly goods, but I am strong inside myself. I have found my inner peace by helping others to search for theirs."

Then Siddhartha knew that he must find his own inner peace. He would become a holy man and he would find a way to end suffering in the world. Siddhartha knew that he must do this even if he had to leave all he loved.

It was late when Siddhartha returned to the palace. Everyone was sleeping, exhausted, for Yashodhara had given birth to their son that day. Softly Siddhartha kissed Yashodhara. She opened her eyes. "I must leave you," he said. Gently he touched the baby's cheek with his finger.

"We shall be with you wherever you are," Yashodhara told him, "and soon we will all be together again."

Spirits came as cushions for his feet and carried Siddhartha silently back to his chariot. With tears he told his driver to take him for his last ride.

Far from the palace, at the edge of a forest, Siddhartha sent his chariot driver home. He continued on foot. He cut off his hair and left his sword at the side of the road. He changed his silken robes for rags and took the heavy golden earrings from his ears. His lobes hung long and loose and empty. He pulled his shoes from his tender feet and began to walk barefoot.

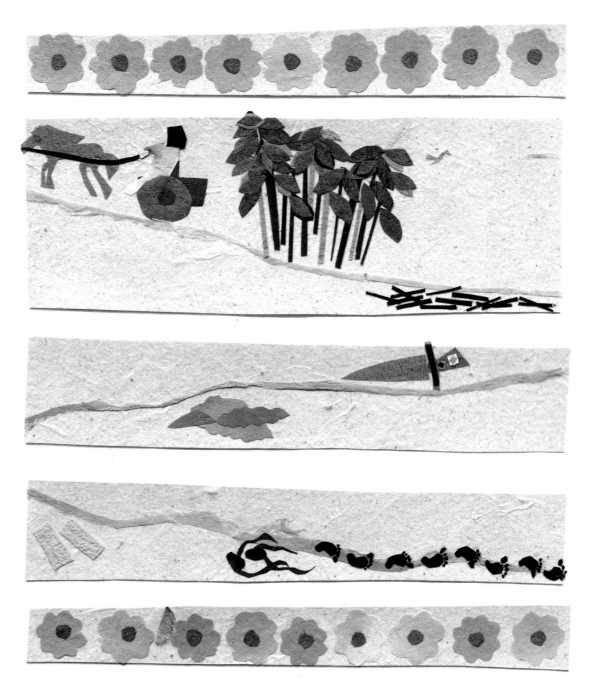

Siddhartha took his
first steps as a
very holy
man.

And so from a wisp of a milky-white elephant, Siddhartha-the-Prince began his way through the eastern world to become Siddhartha-the-Buddha.

AFTERWORD

After renouncing his earthly possessions, Siddhartha spent six years living in the forest, studying and meditating, trying to find his way to understanding or enlightenment. Near the holy city of Benares, India, he delivered his famous Deer Park sermon, which is one of the most sacred events in the history of Buddhism. In this sermon he presented his Noble Eightfold Path and Doctrine of the Four Truths, which are outlines of his philosophies. Siddhartha's way was gentle, kind, and loving. After this sermon, many disciples joined him, including his father, Shuddhodana, his wife, Yashodhara, and their son, Rahula. They now called Siddhartha Buddha (Buddha means the Enlightened One), and worked hard to spread his teachings around the world. When Buddha was eighty-nine years old, he left this world for eternal peace, or Nirvana.

Twenty-five hundred years later, Buddhism is one of the world's major religions, with more than 250 million followers. Throughout its history, Buddhism has been a strong social and cultural, as well as religious, influence in all of Asia. Today it remains vital in many southeast Asian mainland countries, Sri Lanka, Tibet, and Japan. Tales about Buddha have been told in song, story, sculpture, painting, and poetry. Artists have created more images of Buddha than of any other man.

In preparation for writing this book, I studied more than one hundred others. Particularly helpful were *Leaves from the Bodhi Tree* by Susan L. Huntington and John C. Huntington, and *Myths of the Hindus and Buddhists* by Ananda K. Coomaraswamy and Sister Nivedita. I also visited many museums and sacred Buddhist sites. The illustrations rely heavily on historical research as well. The Buddhist manuscript of the Astasāhasrikā Prajñāpāramitā Text, illustrated with water-based pigments painted on talipot palm leaves, was especially inspirational for me and I have tried to share its palette as I made my collages.

Susan L. Roth
Baltimore, Maryland, 1994